WHERE'S SANTA?

ILLUSTRATED BY
CHUCK WHELON

WRITTEN BY BRYONY JONES

DESIGNED BY ANGIE ALLISON AND ZOE BRADLEY

At The North Pole

Welcome to Christmas HQ. Over the past year, Santa and his elves have been hard at work preparing for Christmas. It's all hands on deck. But four days before Christmas, disaster strikes! Ten of Santa's elves have gone missing and, without them, everything in the workshop is getting mixed up. Even the reindeer are trying to help, but they're causing chaos.

Santa has to start a worldwide search for his missing helpers. Can you help him spot the ten missing elves in each picture? See if you can spot Santa in each picture, too. Find the answers plus extra things to spot at the back of the book.

Missing: Elves

Can you help Santa to spot these elves? Look at them carefully, then turn the page and start the search.

Emily
Wrapping Inspector

Zach
Chief Woodworker

Matthew
Reindeer Wrangler

Siobhan
Elf and Safety

Lottie
Battery Installer

Neeta
Address Labeller

Frieda
Novelty-Item Wrapper

Mikey
Elf Resources Manager

Patrice
Shoemaker

Rupert
Chef

A Snowy Village

The elves can sniff out a steaming mug of hot chocolate from far away, and they've followed their noses to this pretty English village on a very frosty evening.

But while the elves are enjoying a huge snowball fight, Santa is trying to stay out of the firing line. Heads up!

Can you pick out Santa and the ten elves?

Safari Sensation

The elves have only ever been to the North Pole Zoo before, and frankly, that's just a shed full of reindeer, so they are amazed by the animals on safari. The giraffes are so tall!

Santa thinks it's too hot. He prefers the cool of the North Pole. And the monkeys won't stop trying to steal his hat.

Can you find Santa and the ten elves?

Christmas Market Mayhem

Santa has followed his mischievous runaway elves to a Christmas market in Germany.

They are enjoying the brightly coloured market stalls, drinking hot cocoa and eating yummy gingerbread.

Can you pick out Santa and the ten elves?

At The Beach

Santa and the elves have made their way to Bondi Beach, in Sydney, Australia.

Santa's not used to the sun at Christmas and he's finding his beard a bit too hot in the scorching summer sun, but the elves are having an amazing time. Surf's up, Dude!

Can you pick out Santa and the ten elves?

Alpine Adventure

Anyone for skiing? At a popular resort in France, the elves are clicking on their skis and testing their skills on the slopes. Let's hope they're not afraid of heights!

The cold is turning Santa's nose as red as Rudolph's. He's really not a fan of extreme sports.

Can you pick out Santa and the ten elves?

Santas Galore

The elves are confused. Why is there a whole room of people dressed up like Santa? It's a Santa Convention, that's why.

Santa wonders if anyone would like to take his place back at the North Pole HQ. It's hard work getting everything ready for Christmas.

Can you spot the real Santa and his missing ten elves?

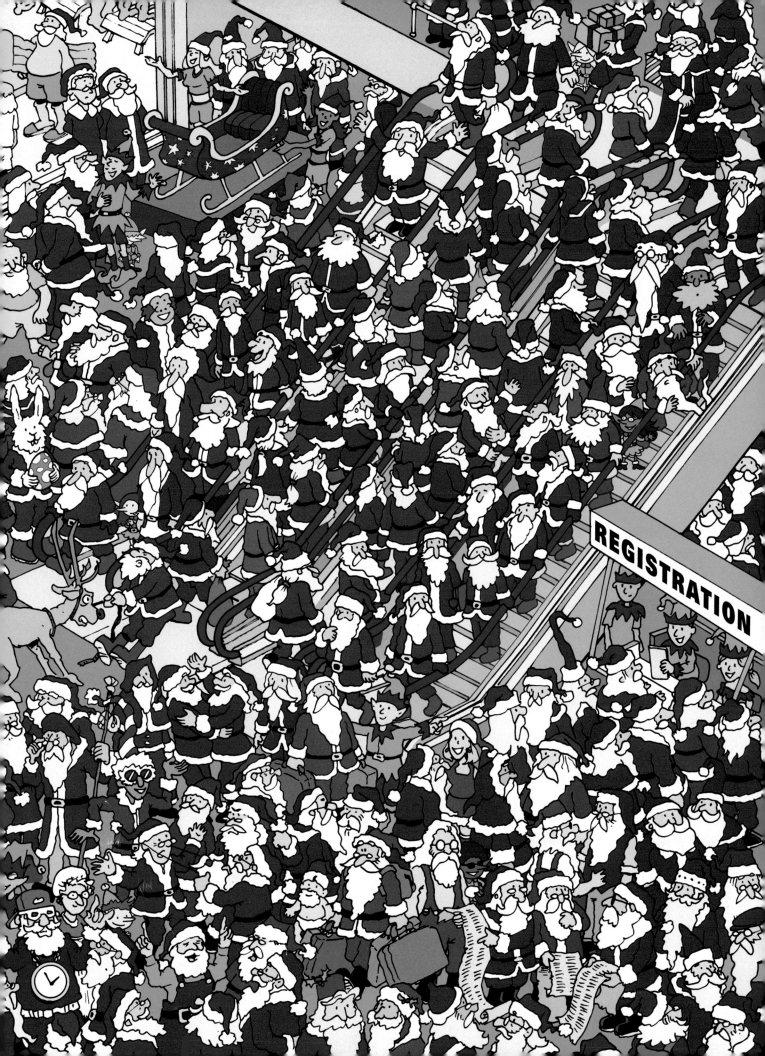

REGISTRATION

Family Feast

The elves are stuffed. They've eaten turkey, goose, and more roast potatoes than there are reindeer in the North Pole. But Santa, well, he's just getting started.

He loves to see the kids' faces when they unwrap their presents. It makes all that hard work in the run up to Christmas worth it.

Can you spot Santa and the ten elves?

At The Ballet

The audience is hushed, the stage lights are up, and Santa's marvelling at what's unfolding on the stage. There are leaps, jumps and pirouettes aplenty.

The elves are keen to learn a few moves so they can show off at the annual elf disco.

Can you pick out Santa and the ten elves?

Festive Fiesta!

The elves love a good party, so it's no surprise that they've travelled to São Paulo in Brazil.

Amazed by all the colourful costumes and twinkling lights, the elves are lost in the festivities. But with everybody in costume, it's even harder for Santa to find them.

Can you pick out Santa and the ten elves?

Ice Skating

The elves have decided to check out the fabulous ice rink at the Rockefeller Center in New York City.

Santa finds the ice much too slippery and prefers to stay on the sidelines but the elves want to be right in the middle of the action, showing off their moves by spinning and twirling gracefully.

Can you pick out Santa and the ten elves?

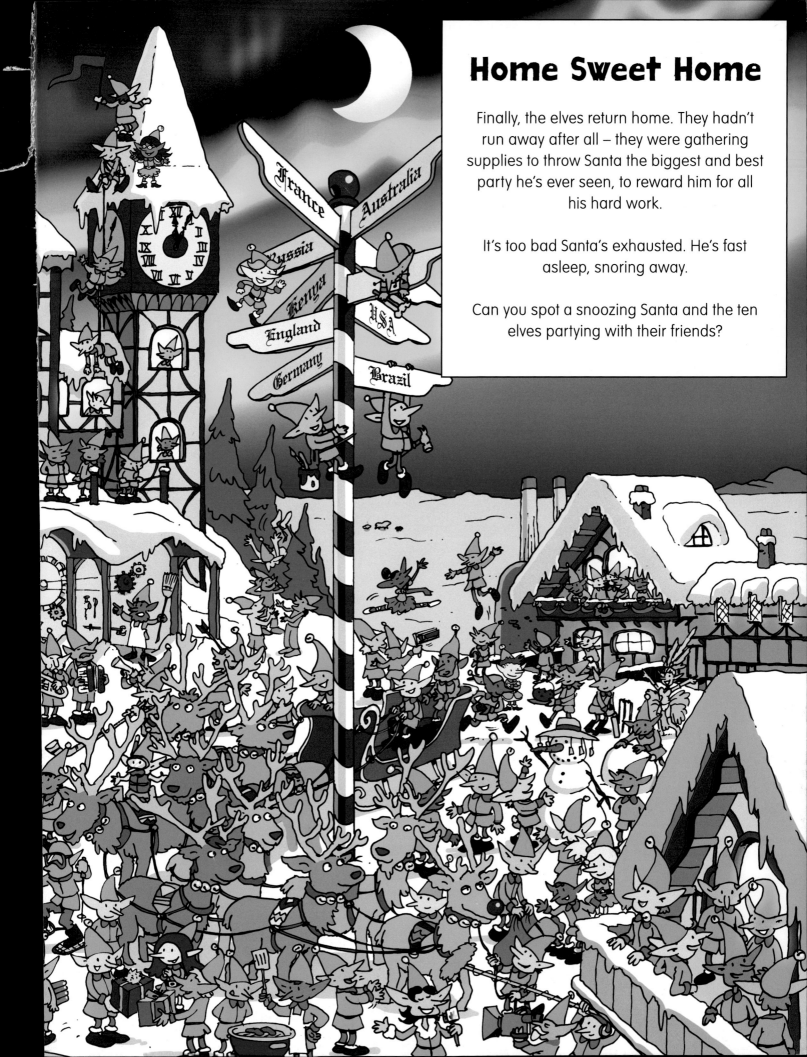

Home Sweet Home

Finally, the elves return home. They hadn't run away after all – they were gathering supplies to throw Santa the biggest and best party he's ever seen, to reward him for all his hard work.

It's too bad Santa's exhausted. He's fast asleep, snoring away.

Can you spot a snoozing Santa and the ten elves partying with their friends?

ANSWERS

Spotter's Checklist

Carol singers ☐

Someone falling through the ice ☐

A man dressed as a crocodile ☐

A badger ☐

Someone being hit in the face by a snowball ☐

A Snowy Village

Safari Sensation

Spotter's Checklist

A crocodile dentist ☐

A punk zebra ☐

A big cat pretending to be Rudolph ☐

A monkey with a bell ☐

An ostrich being ridden ☐

Spotter's Checklist

Someone being electrocuted ☐

A skiier in the wrong place ☐

Two people dressed as snowmen ☐

A donkey sitting on a horse ☐

A thief ☐

Christmas Market Mayhem

At The Beach

Spotter's Checklist

Two crustaceans pulling a cracker ☐

A jellyfish on someone's head ☐

Ouch! Someone who's just sat on a porcupine ☐

A cricket ball in a Christmas pudding ☐

Two sandmen ☐

Spotter's Checklist

A rocket-powered skiier ☐

Someone falling out of a lift ☐

A human snowball ☐

Someone with two broken legs ☐

Someone skiing backwards ☐

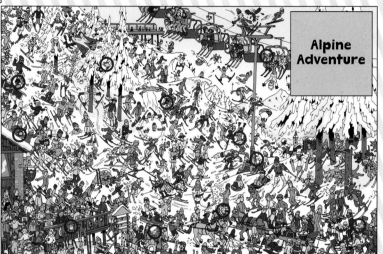

Alpine Adventure

Santas Galore

Spotter's Checklist

A reindeer who's reluctant to ride the escalator ☐

A Santa doing a bomb into the pool ☐

A baby Santa ☐

An Easter-bunny Santa ☐

A Santa with a chimney on his head ☐

Spotter's Checklist

Someone dressed as a fairy ☐

Someone with an arrow on their forehead ☐

A girl wearing a fake moustache ☐

A cracker being pulled ☐

Someone licking a candy cane ☐

Family Feast

At The Ballet

Spotter's Checklist

A vampire ☐

A dangling sandwich ☐

A pea shooter ☐

A pirate hat in the audience ☐

A telescope ☐

Spotter's Checklist

Someone doing the limbo ☐

A man with pineapples on his hat ☐

A dog on the back of a motorbike ☐

A drummer with a whistle ☐

A trumpet player riding a horse ☐

Festive Fiesta!

Ice Skating

Spotter's Checklist

A flying superhero ☐

A film crew ☐

Someone dressed as the Statue of Liberty ☐

An Audrey Hepburn lookalike ☐

Someone wearing a panda hat ☐

Spotter's Checklist

An elf in a carnival costume ☐

Two puppet elves ☐

An elf wearing a scuba mask ☐

A flying elf ☐

A snowboarding elf ☐

Home Sweet Home